Ladybird Readers

The Big Fish
Activity Book

Activities written by Coleen Degnan-Veness

Chant on page 16 written by Pippa Mayfield

Illustrated by Chris Jevons

 Singing *  Reading  Speaking

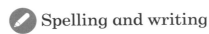 Spelling and writing 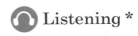 Listening *

* To complete these activities, listen to tracks 3–8 of the audio download available at www.ladybird.com/ladybirdreaders

1 Listen and repeat. Trace. *

1

2

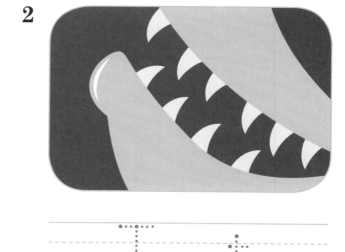

T t

3

4

A a

* To complete this activity, listen to track 3 of the audio download available at **www.ladybird.com/ladybirdreaders**

1

ph

2

ay

3

ai

4

ea

3 Look. Listen and color in the correct sounds. *

1

ar	ai	ea

2

t	s	m

3

ar	or	ay

4

s	t	a

 * To complete this activity, listen to track 5 of the audio download available at **www.ladybird.com/ladybirdreaders**

Look and say. Match. 🗨

1

sail

2

teeth

s　　t

3

tail

4

sea

5

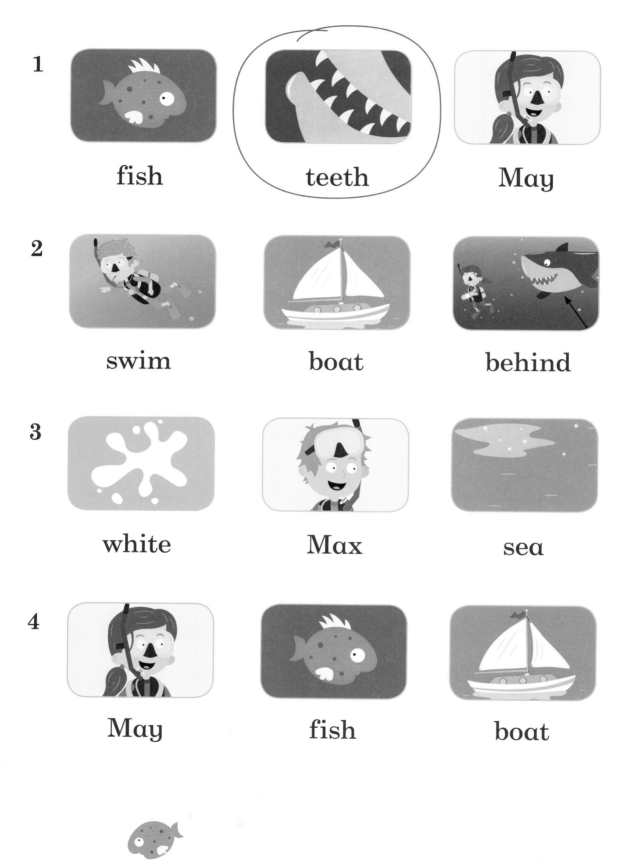

1

fish

teeth

May

2

swim

boat

behind

3

white

Max

sea

4

May

fish

boat

6 Look and say. Find the words.

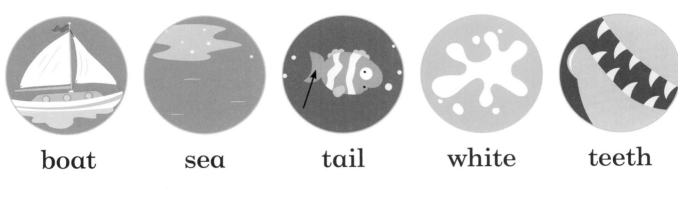

boat   sea   tail   white   teeth

ayboatwhseabrtailchwhiteprteethsp

7 Read and say the words. Match.

1 Max

2 May

3 tail

4 sail

5 sea

8 Look. What can you see?
Put a ✓ or a ✗ in the boxes.

1 take a photo

2 May

3 boat

4 long tail

5 teeth

9 Look and read. Circle the correct words.

1

What a very long **sail!** / (**tail!**)

2

I am taking a **fish.** / **photo**.

3

Don't **worry.** / **sorry**.

4

I don't want to **eat** / **sea** you.

10 **Look. Circle the words with the same sound.**
Say the words.

1 May  (say) sea

2 sail  Max tail

3 boat  coat long

4 sea  take eat

5 white  fish bite

11 **Look and read. Circle *yes* or *no*.**

1 Max and May find some fish. (yes) no

2 Max and May can swim. yes no

3 May sees a boat. yes no

4 Max takes a photo. yes no

5 The fish with the long tail
   eats May. yes no

12 Look. Circle the correct words and write them on the lines. 📖 ✏️

1

behind   from

A very big fish swims _____ behind _____ May.

2

swim   eat

"May! That big fish wants to _____ YOU!"

3

boat   fish

Max and May swim to the _____.

13 Say the words. Match, and write the words on the lines. 🗨 ✏️

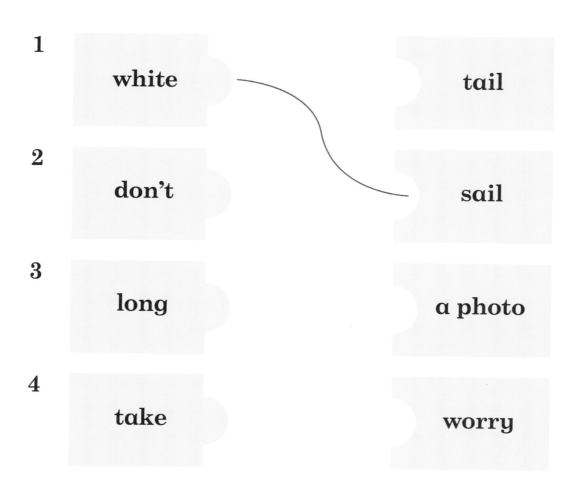

1   white

2   don't

3   long

4   take

tail

sail

a photo

worry

1 .... white .... sail

2 ....

3 ....

4 ....

14 Listen. Write the words. *

1 Max likes the ⎯⎯⎯ sea ⎯⎯⎯.

2 I can ⎯⎯⎯⎯⎯ with the fish!

3 What a nice ⎯⎯⎯⎯⎯!

4 ⎯⎯⎯⎯⎯ likes the sea, too.

* To complete this activity, listen to track 7 of the audio download available at www.ladybird.com/ladybirdreaders

15 Say the chant. *

s s s s

s in swim,

s in swim.

t t t-t-t

t in teeth,

t in teeth.

ea ea ea ea

ea in sea,

ea in sea.

ai ai ai ai

ai in tail,

ai in tail.

* To complete this activity, listen to track 8 of the audio download available at **www.ladybird.com/ladybirdreaders**